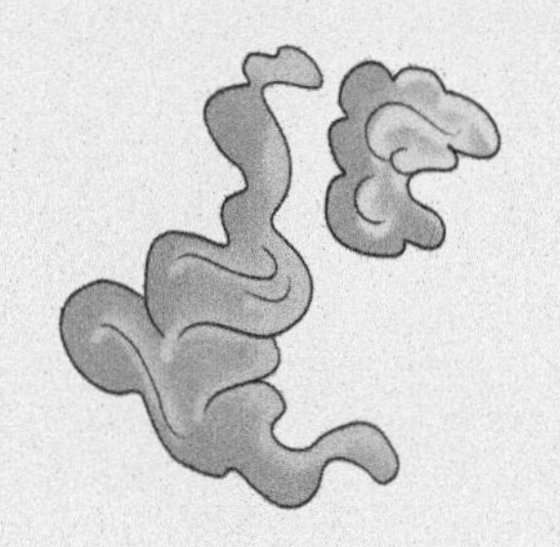

The Cotton Candy Kid

Jacqueline McComas

Illustrated by Susan Shorter

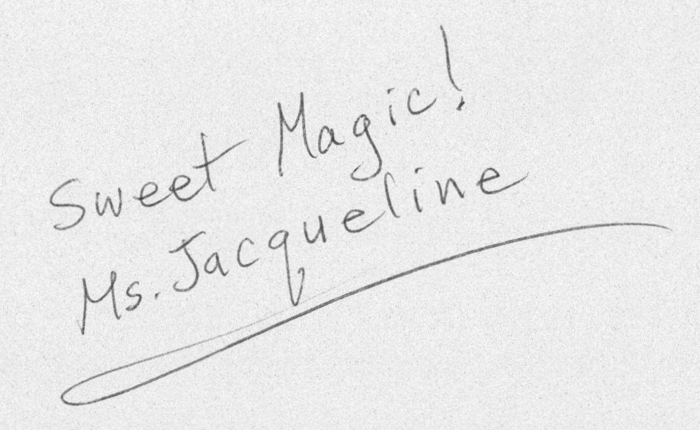

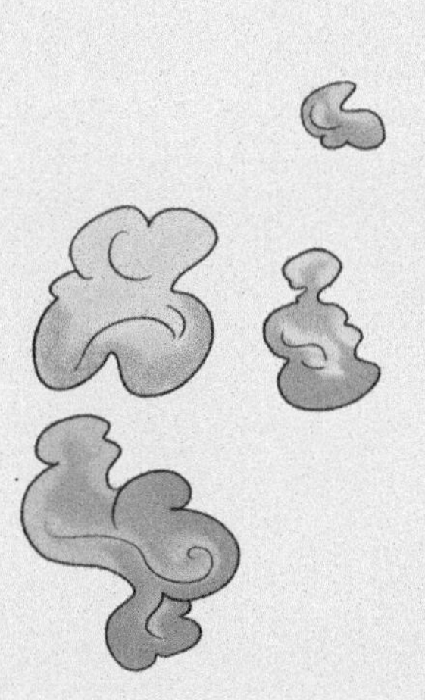

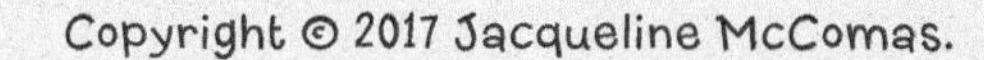

Archway Publishing books may be ordered through booksellers or by contacting:

Archway Publishing
1663 Liberty Drive
Bloomington, IN 47403
www.archwaypublishing.com
1 (888) 242-5904

ISBN: 978-1-4808-4195-6 (sc)
ISBN: 978-1-4808-4196-3 (e)

Print information available on the last page.

Archway Publishing rev. date: 2/8/2017

COTTON
CANDY

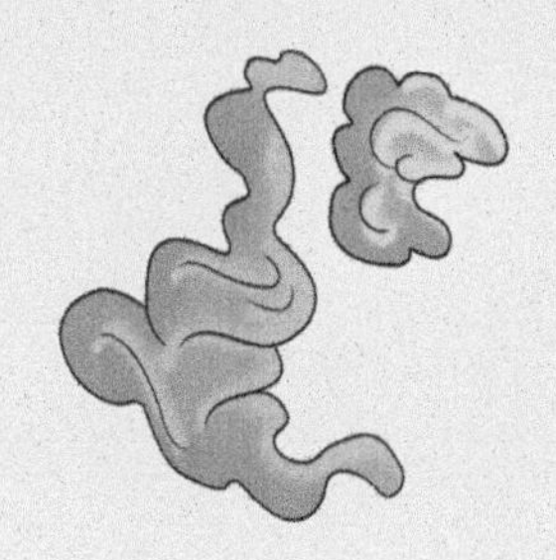

If anyone loved cotton candy, it was Casey.

From the very first time he saw the big, pink swirls of spun sugar at the circus, Casey wanted to try some.

It tasted like a fluffy, sweet cloud to him. But, before he could munch on it, it disappeared in his mouth - just like magic.

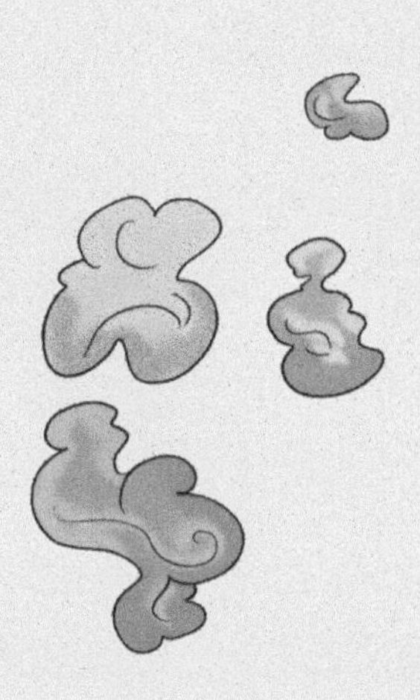

COTTON
CANDY

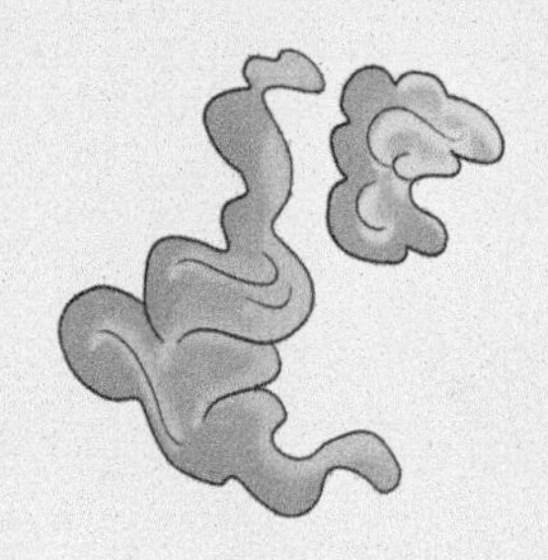

To Casey, cotton candy was the "best" candy in the whole wide world!

He loved it so much, his parents bought him an old, used cotton candy machine.

And soon, he was doing all kinds of tricks with the cotton candy. He twirled it, bent it, stretched it, squeezed it, and rolled it.

He even made yummy "Cotton Candy Sandwiches" for his family and friends.

Everyone started to call him the Cotton Candy Kid.

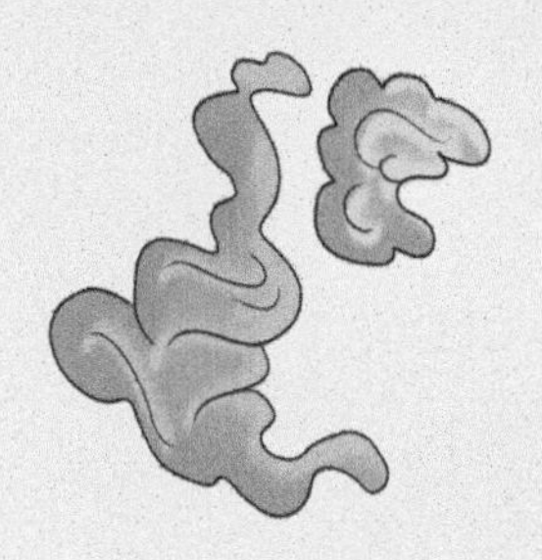

One morning, after a heavy rainfall, the Cotton Candy Kid heard a horn beeping and beeping and his little brother shouting and shouting, "Help! Help!" His brother Zack was in his car and the tires were stuck in a big mud puddle.

The Cotton Candy Kid quickly made a chain of green cotton candy, aimed it, and proudly said,

"Cotton candy, cotton candy, very sweet and always handy!"

He twirled and swirled his cotton candy chain around the entire car and pulled his little brother out of the mud.

"Good job," shouted Zack as he waved goodbye and sped away.

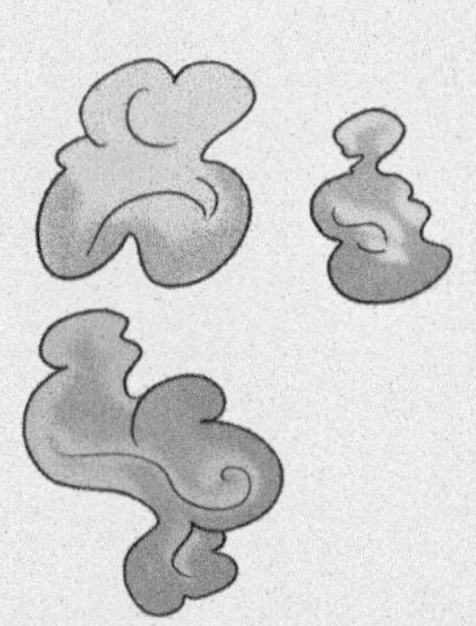

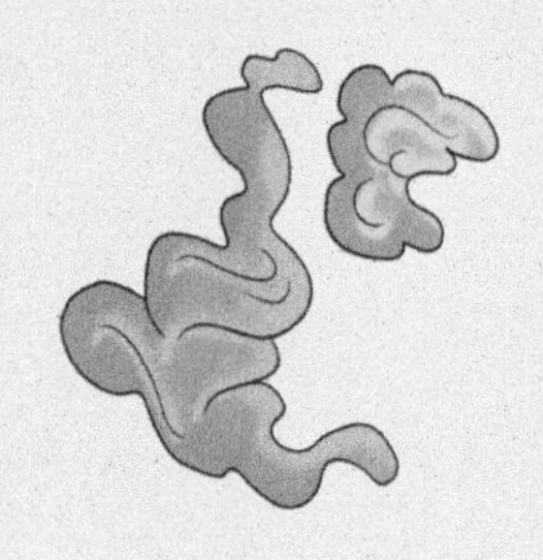

“Giddyup, giddyup,” said the Cotton Candy Kid as he rode his horse through the tall grass. It was then that he looked over and saw a giraffe running down the street. He wondered where he came from. Did he escape from the zoo?

The Cotton Candy Kid immediately made a long, strong rope of blue cotton candy, made a loop at one end, and proudly said,

“Cotton candy, cotton candy, very sweet and always handy!”

He lassoed the cotton candy around the neck of the running giraffe and instantly, the giraffe stopped in his tracks.

The zookeeper, running after the giraffe, yelled out, “Thanks for catching Geronimo. I think he ran off to buy a new hat.”

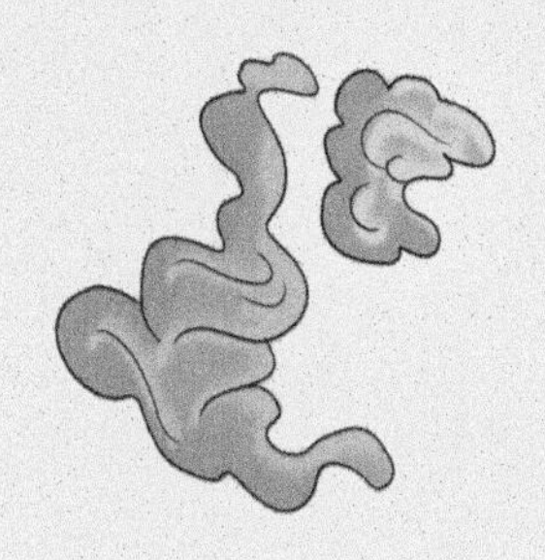

The Cotton Candy Kid and his brother Zack were playing ball in the backyard with twin friends, Cindy and Mindy. They heard a kitten crying from a tree top, "Meow, meow, meow." It couldn't get down.

Cotton Candy Kid rushed over and made a sliding board of yellow cotton candy. He placed it up against the tree and proudly said,

"Cotton candy, cotton candy, very sweet and always handy!"

The kitten slowly walked down the sweet, cotton candy slide.

"Our hero," said Cindy and Mindy.

"Good job," said Zack.

"Meow," purred the happy kitten.

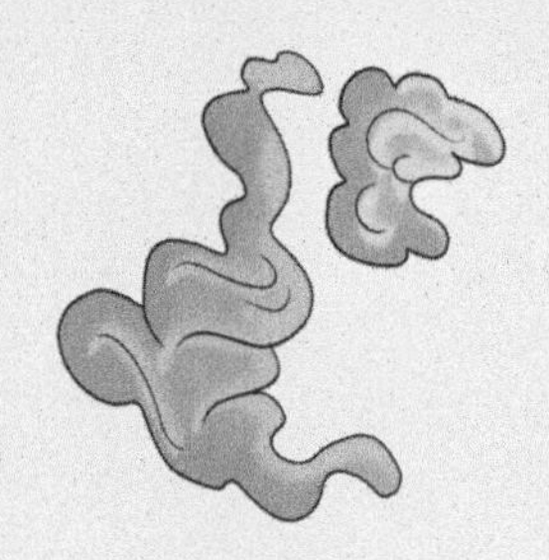

Every day, the Cotton Candy Kid continued to use more and more and more cotton candy.

He made colorful swings for his neighborhood friends and fixed a broken bridge over a small stream.

The more cotton candy he used, the more the cotton candy machine made! He wondered if the machine would ever stop.

And as usual, the cotton candy kept sticking to him and sticking to him until...

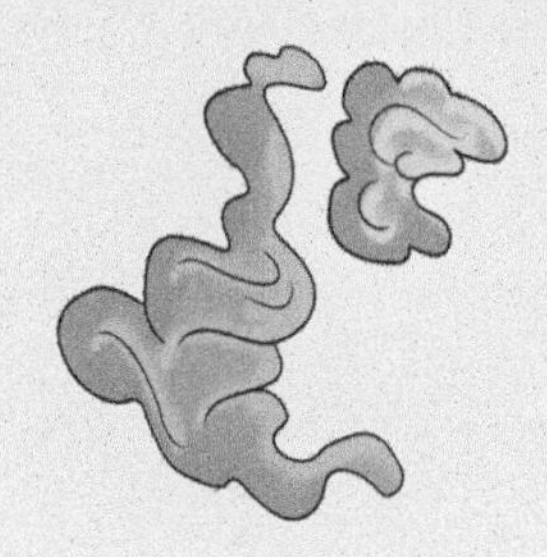

Until the cotton candy stuck to him so much, he looked like a...

COTTON CANDY MONSTER!

And, if you listened very carefully, you might have heard him mumble,

“Yum, yum, I wove my totton tandy -- very tweet and always dandy!”

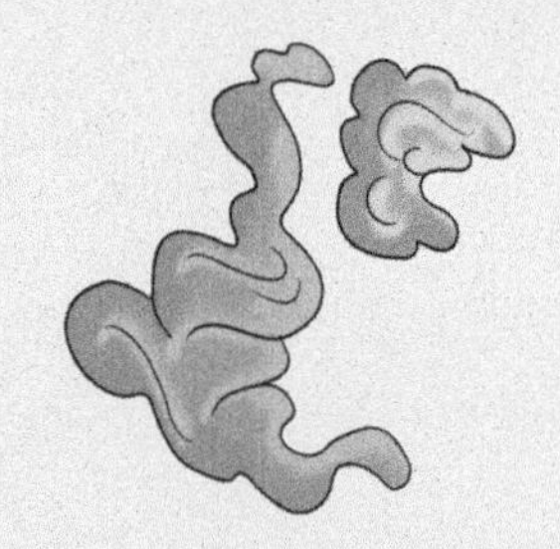

THE END

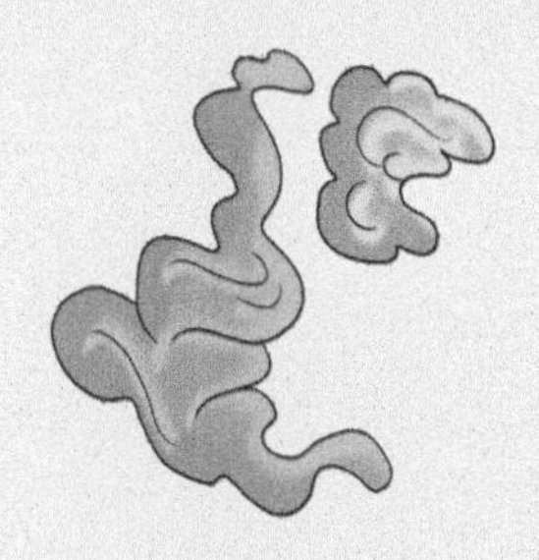

COTTON CANDY

Cotton candy is also called candy floss, fairy floss, or spun sugar.

Cotton candy is made of air and sugar with food coloring and flavoring.

One scrumptious serving weighs less than an ounce or a balloon. Wow!

Cotton candy is usually sold on a paper cone or baton from a vending machine at carnivals and fairs. But it is also sold pre-packaged in supermarkets and other stores.

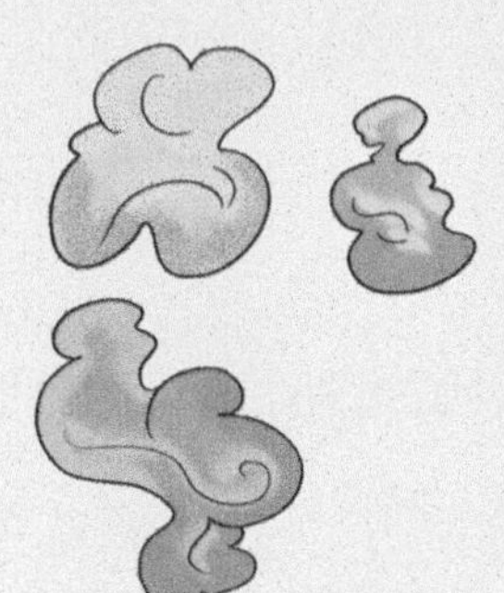

RECIPE

(Adult supervision is required)

CASEY'S "COTTON CANDY" SANDWICHES

This recipe makes 6 sandwiches.

1 to 2 ounces or 1/4 cup <u>white</u> chocolate wafers, candy melts, or chips

1 stack of Ritz crackers or 12 crackers

1 new package of cotton candy with assorted flavors and colors

1. Melt the white chocolate.
2. Place 12 crackers, flat side up, on table; place a very small dollop of warm, melted white chocolate on the top of each cracker.
3. Place a small piece of fluffy cotton candy on top of the dollop of white chocolate.
4. Cover cotton candy crackers with remaining 6 crackers, flat side down. Best served warm, immediately.
5. Enjoy the crunchy cracker, the warm creamy white chocolate, and the magic of cotton candy!

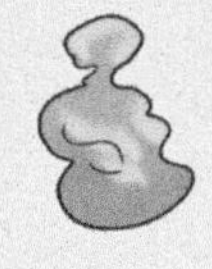

Original recipe by Jacqueline McComas, 2015

CPSIA information can be obtained
at www.ICGtesting.com
Printed in the USA
BVOW05s2003210217
476544BV00008B/5/P